PUFFIN BOOKS
Published by the Penguin Group Penguin Putnam Books for Young Readers,
345 Hudson Street, New York, New York 10014, U.S.A.
Penguin Books Ltd, 27 Wrights Lane, London W8 5TZ, England
Penguin Books Australia Ltd, Ringwood, Victoria, Australia
Penguin Books Canada Ltd, 10 Alcorn Avenue, Toronto, Ontario, Canada M4V 3B2
Penguin Books (N.Z.) Ltd, 182-190 Wairau Road, Auckland 10, New Zealand

Penguin Books Ltd, Registered Offices: Harmondsworth, Middlesex, England

Published by Puffin Books,
a division of Penguin Putnam Books for Young Readers, 2001

10 9 8 7 6 5 4 3 2

TM & © 2001 DreamWorks
Text by Dr. R. E. Volting
Illustrations by Lawrence Hamashima
Book design by Jim Hoover

All rights reserved

Puffin Books ISBN 0-14-131261-0

Printed in the United States of America

DREAMWORKS™

# Shrek

## Gag Book

### by Dr. R. E. Volting

### Illustrations by Lawrence Hamashima

Today's weather: Humid and muggy with a slight chance of locusts—another perfect day!

Engraving © Pap. A. Razzi

# DEAR DONKEY

## Advice to the Lovelorn and Dull-Witted

Dear Donkey:
I am interested in a mangy, loud, four-legged creature who won't even look at me. I'm well-built (approximately thirteen tons) but light on my feet, with a twenty-yard wingspan. Okay, my skin is a bit scaly, and my breath has been known to scorch small seaside villages, but I have my own castle and I love to travel. What can I do to win him over?

—Anonymous

↪

**NOTHING!** You're a Dragon! Leave me alone— I mean, Dear Anonymous, some loves are not meant to be. Sounds like you have a big imagination. Use it.

The Fifth of August in the Year of Our Lord Eight Hundred Forty-Two

# CLASSIFIEDS

**For Sale:**
Seeds. Will grow immediately. Biggest results you have ever seen or your money back. All sales final.
Contact jack@beanstalk.com.

**Help wanted:**
Horses and men. Auxiliary force needed IMMEDIATELY for emergency massive cleanup. Surgical reattachment skills welcome.
Contact king@humpty.wall.

**Jobs wanted:**
Seven strong men—caring, humble, work together well. Skills include woodworking, heavy lifting, singing. Shorter than Lord Farquaad (a plus for public relations work).
Write 7dwrfs@duLoc.woods

# Shrek Happens!

What is an ogre's favorite flying machine?

A hurl-icopter!

Who is Shrek's favorite singer?

Frank Snotra!

# Shrek's ABCs

**A** is for Armpit, O sweetest perfume,

**B** is for Belching, to clear any room,

**C** is for Crusty, a fine way to be,

**D** is Disgust, which I offer to thee.

**E** is for Eggs, very tasty when spoiled,

**F** is for Flies, eaten fresh, fried, or broiled,

**G** is for Gross, a word like "Disgusting,"

**H** is for Hurl, which you do when you're busting.

**I** is for Ignorant Donkey beside me,

**J** is for Jackass—alas, woe betide me!

**K** is for King, who resembles a stump,

**L** is for Land of DuLoc (what a dump!),

**M** is for Mashing that Farquaad to pulp,

**N** is for Nibbling him down, gulp by gulp.

**O** is for Ogre,
alone and ignored,

**P** is for Princess,
admired and adored,

**Q** is for Quietly
storming her castle,

**R** is for Rescuing her
(what a hassle!).

**S** is for Slithering,
fire-breathing beast,

**T** is to Try not to become
its dinner feast,

U is for Underwear burnt by its breath,

V is for Very close brush against death,

W is for Wow, the beast digs on Ol' Mule!

X is for X-cellent break, very cool.

Y is a "Yahoo!" for triumphs just passed,

Z? Zesty zephyrs of digestive gas!

What is the Three Blind Mice's favorite game?

**Hide-and-Squeak!**

What squeaks, likes cheese, and goes *thump-thump-thump* against the pantry wall?

**Three blind mice!**

# Swamp Cafe

## Unappetizers

Tossed-Cookie Salad
Cream of Brain Soup
Mixed Spleen Salad
Hominy Guts

## Main coarse

Cheeseboogers
Western Vomlette
Spaghetti with Hairballs and Sweat Sauce
Sour and Sour Chicken
Cold Dogs (extra charge if dog is still hot)
Roadkill Wraps

Shrimp-skin Cocktail
Fried Eyeball Nuggets
Earwax Beans

# Blecchxtras

*French Flies*

*Rat-atooey (dietary substitute made with Three Blind Mice)*

*Mashed Sweat Potatoes*

*Potatoes Auuugh-Rotten*

*Lice Peel-Off*

# Fluids

*Bodily (Regular or Decapitated)*

*Green Tea (Win a free dessert if you correctly guess why it's green!)*

*Hot Sneeze Toddy*

# Aftershocks

*Mice Cream Sundae*

*Lice Pudding*

*Mucus Cakes*

*Fartune Cookies*

*Pickin' Pie (Nose or Toenail)*

**Shrek:** What did you get that little medal for?

**Donkey:** For singing.

**Shrek:** What did you get the big one for?

**Donkey:** For stopping.

What do donkeys put on the fire at Christmas?

A Mule log!

"I'm a Donkey on the edge!"

What is Donkey's favorite sport?

Basketball, because he's a good dribbler!

# Gutbuster Video

**Overdue Notice for Customer:** Shrek

**The following items are overdue and
must be returned as soon as possible:**

*Beauty and the Belch*

*Pukémon*

*Richie Retch*

*Eccccchs Men*

*Old Smeller*

*The Gizzard of Oz*

*Splatman*

—You have a
friend in DuLoc

4½¢

Shrek the Ogre

The Swamp

Outside DuLoc

Engraving © Pap A. Razzi

# DEAR DONKEY

## Advice to the Lovelorn and Dull-Witted

Dear Donkey:
How do you get rid of a mangy barnyard animal that won't shut up, is scared of its own shadow, and sticks to you like glue?
—Shrek the Ogre

Dear Shrek,
Wait a minute, Rat Breath. You can't fool me. I know what you're talking about. And for your information, a dragon is not a barnyard animal.

❧

Dear Donkey,
Everybody teases me. They tell me I'm made of wood. But I'm not— I'm a real boy! I am. Really, really, really, I AM a real boy! I mean it!
—Pinocchio

Dear Termite Magnet,
If you're a real boy, then I'm a noble steed. Maybe you'd better see a shrink. Or a carpenter.

Donkey: Hey Shrek, why are your fingers always in your nose?

Shrek: I'm jealous, I guess.

Donkey: Jealous? Of who?

Shrek: Peter Piper. He picked a peck of pickled peppers!

**Donkey:** Lord Farquaad comes upon an old friend in the woods. The friend says four words, and Farquaad sentences him to death.

**Shrek:** What did the friend say?

**Donkey:** "Small world, isn't it?"

What is Shrek's favorite basketball move?

A **slime** dunk!

**Gluttony** is the best policy.

Time flies when you're eating flies.

# WORDS TO LIVE BY

The hair is always greener in another man's nose.

Girls DO make **passes** at guys who pass **gasses**.

Early to bed, early to rise makes Shrek a dull boy.

Everybody likes parfaits.

What do you call Princess Fiona when she's using a broom?

Sweeping Beauty!

What did Fiona say to the photographer?

**Someday my prints will come!**

What happens to Princess Fiona when the sun goes down?

**She turns into Sleeping Ugly!**

# Shrek's
## Totally Disgusting
## but Utterly True
## Gross Facts Trivia Quiz!

**1.** Three-quarters of house-
hold dust is made of:
a) dead skin cells
b) bacteria
c) very small stones

**2.** One-fifth of all
methane gas emissions on
this planet comes from:

a) the catalytic breakdown
of fossil fuels
b) morning mouth
c) insect farts

**3.** Sweat contains the same chemical compound as in the fluid commonly known as:

a) dinitrophenylketonuria
b) chocolate milk
c) urine

**4.** The tendency to fart a lot runs in families.

**True or false?**

**5.** The gastric-breeding frog gives birth by:

a) hopping up and down vigorously
b) lying on its back in a warm pond
c) vomiting out its young

**6. Another phrase for nose-picking is:**

a) circumnostrilocution
b) hunt and peck
c) rhinotillexomanin

**7. Approximately how many miles an hour does a fart travel?**

a) 7
b) 26
c) None. No fart travels for a whole hour.

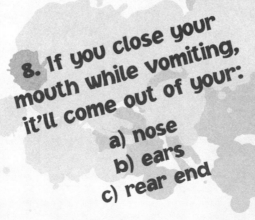

**8. If you close your mouth while vomiting, it'll come out of your:**

a) nose
b) ears
c) rear end

**9.** An average person produces enough spit in a lifetime to:

a) fill a swimming pool 10 feet wide, 15 feet long, and 5 1/2 feet deep

b) equal the amount of water used by an average person in one month

c) both of the above

**10.** The more you burp, the less you fart.
**True or false?**

Under what category will you find Lord Farquaad's biography?

Short stories!

If Lord Farquaad were in the World Series, what would he play?

Shortstop!

What is Lord Farquaad's main health problem?

Shortness of breath!

What does Lord Farquaad sit on?

A booster throne!

What kind of chef works in Lord Farquaad's Royal Kitchen?

A short-order cook!

# Welcome to DULOC

## Rules of the Kingdom

### DON'T make waves
Except from left to right in the royal
stadium, to cheer the arrival of Lord Farquaad.

### DON'T spit
But flinch not when Lord Farquaad spitteth on you.

### DO always stay in line
So that Lord Farquaad may create a
pleasing domino effect with one swift kick.

### DO keep off the grass
Unless testing it, with bare feet, for little
doggie surprises before use by Lord Farquaad.

### DO keep your eyes below
### Lord Farquaad's at all times
Kneepads available at the Castle Concierge Office.

### DO have a great time!
Void where prohibited; happiness may not exceed
that of Lord Farquaad under penalty of death.

# Shrek's recipe cards

## The Eyes Have It

**Procedure:**
Roll eyeballs in toe jam and fresh-picked dandruff.
Place in container of squashed fly juice.
Allow to pickle for three days.
Chill and serve as special dessert treat.
(High protein content!)

## Stubbornly Good Donkey Burgers

**Needed:**
One donkey
Bow and arrow
Matches

**Procedure:**
Find donkey in woods.
With bow and arrow, hunt down like dog.

flame for one hour.
Serve with parsley.
Add butter.

**HEY! CUT THAT OUT!**

What do you get when
a dragon sneezes?

Out of the way!

How do you know if there's
a dragon under your bed?

Your nose hits the ceiling!

What
does a
giant fire-
breathing
dragon
eat?

Anything
she wants!

Donkey: Knock, knock.

Shrek: Who's there?

Donkey: Juan.

Shrek: Juan who?

Donkey: Juan a nice big parfait?

Shrek: Knock, knock.

Donkey: Who's there?

Shrek: Alec.

Donkey: Alec who?

Shrek: Alec onions better.

Where are ogre children educated?

In **smell**-ementary schools!

What kind of journals do they write in?

Decomposition notebooks!

**W**hat two things are necessary for a sumptuous witch's meal?

Hansel and griddle!

**W**ho plays the flute, lures kids through the town, and slithers?

The Pied Viper!

**W**ho is Mother Goose's favorite actor?

Tom Honks!

**W**hy did Humpty-
Dumpty have a
great fall?

To make up for
a lousy summer!

**W**hat does Shrek
get after a long jog
around the swamp
on a hot day?

Pus in boots!

**Massive arms**
Can headlock
**eight**
knights
at a time!

**Onion breath**
Brings tears
to the eyes
of anyone
who comes
too close!

**Toxic**
toe cheese
Knocks
opponents
out cold!

**Farts**
of fury
Blast
competitors
out of the
ring!

What kind of doctor does Lord Farquaad see once a week?

**A shrink!**

What is Lord Farquaad's cook's specialty?

**Shortbread!**

What kind of underwear does Lord Farquaad wear?

**Briefs!**

**Knight:** The lord fired me today.

**Fiona:** Why?

**Knight:** I can't figure it out. He always looked up to me.

# What's Your 👹-IQ?
## Take the
## Ogre Intelligence Quiz

**1. When facing a swamp-to-swamp salesman, do you:**

a) politely ask him in?
b) close the door on his face?
c) threaten to cut open his kidneys and drink the fluids for lunch?

**2. If your house smells like rotted flesh, animal waste, and farts, do you:**

a) open the windows and let in some air?
b) move?
c) take great pride in yourself?

**3.** While walking in the swamp, you see a pack of vultures eating a dead possum. Do you:

a) chase after them with a pitchfork?
b) think deep, sad thoughts about the food chain and what it implies about the world?
c) flex those fingers and dig in?

**4.** After walking through the swamp on a hot day, it feels best to:

a) relax with a soft drink and crackers
b) sit in the sun and watch the plant life decay
c) remove your shoes, sniff deeply, then lick insoles

**5.** Another word for "festering fly larvae" is

a) maggots
b) pupa
c) lunch

If you answered c to all of the above, congratulations! You're a true Doctor of Disgust, Gourmet of Grossness, and credit to crassness—a real ogre!

# Eat, Stink, and be Scary

What are long and green and usually found in an ogre's ears?

**His fingers!**

What does an ogre like on his toast?

**Toe jam!**

What does the ogre judge say?

**"Odor in the court!"**

# More Incredible Disgusting-but-True Trivia

The average person burps fifteen times a day.

The mouth contains 250 different types of bacteria.

Meat contains chemicals that lead to smellier farts.

A baby creates thirty-eight gallons of drool in its first year of life.

Eating beets turns your urine red.

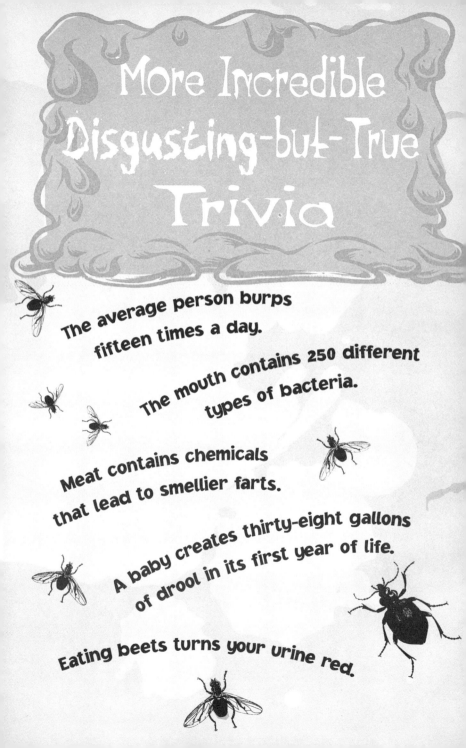

# Cockroach Corner:

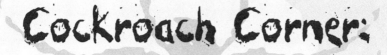

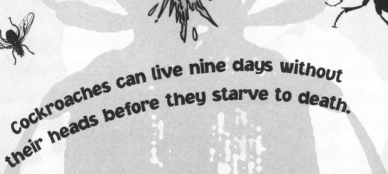

Cockroaches can live nine days without their heads before they starve to death.

Cockroaches continue to fart for eighteen minutes after they die.

Cockroaches fart every fifteen minutes.

What is a
dragon's favorite
breakfast treat?

Shredded feet!

What should you do
if you find a dragon
in your house?

Find somewhere else to live!

What has a spiked tail,
plates on its back, sixteen
wheels, and breathes fire?

A dragon on
roller skates!

What's the best way
to talk to a dragon?
Long-distance!

Why do dragons have long necks?
Because their
feet smell!

You're a beautiful princess locked in a tall tower. Pick your rescuer:

A smelly, green, uncouth ogre with a great personality
**OR**
A shrimpy, egotistical lord with the keys to the kingdom

# It's bedtime—pick one:

A big, wet bedtime kiss from
Dragon's larger-than-life lips
## OR
Sharing a tent with Shrek after a
campfire meal of spoiled skunk
with rancid beans

# You're a cookie with some valuable information, about to be interrogated by an uncaring creep.
# What do you pick?

Being dunked in a glass
of ice-cold milk
## OR
Having your gum-
drop buttons (and
other extremities)
plucked off one
by one

## Pick one item for your holiday stocking:

Brimstone incense
**OR**
Eau de Wet
Donkey
Fur cologne

## You're the Magic Mirror. Pick one:

Lord Farquaad's
bedroom wall
**OR**
Shrek's out-
house wall

# You're on a dinner date with a special someone. Pick one:

The Princess's Pu Pu Platter: freshly spun "cotton candy" made from spiderwebs and partially digested flying insects

**OR**

Shrek's Swamp-Surprise Stew: fermented swamp water, juice of porcupine pustules, and eyeballs du jour

QUICK PICKS

Mud shower
**OR**
Bug-gut
toothpaste

Fish-eye tartare
**OR**
Weedrat stew

# An Ode to Odor

A **belch** is but a
gust of wind,
that cometh
from the heart.
But should it take
a downward trend,
It turns

into a
**Fart.**